Princess the Toad

Written and illustrated by
Simon Jamie

ISBN 978-0-9573309-3-1

FINGERMOUSE
BOOKS
www.fingermousebooks.com

To Larissa
Enjoy!

With thanks to
Isla Jamie
for her amazing ideas

And to **Owen Jamie** *for*
his illustration improvements

Contents

Introduction

About toads who aren't princesses

This is not a story about a princess. At least, not at the beginning—I hope the title didn't make you think it was. It's actually a story about a toad who happened to be called Princess. The picture on the cover of the book might have given this away, or at least given you a clue.

The toad in question was the only daughter of Mr and Mrs Toad, who had no real names of their own as they were quite ordinary toads. Most toads don't bother having names because they're quite busy enough with the business of being toads— to a toad, a name is usually just another thing to worry about.

However, because they only had one child, Mr and Mrs Toad had decided to do something very unusual and give their daughter a name. They didn't actually know any names, otherwise they might have called her Jane, or Matilda or something more name-like. Instead they named her Princess, as it seemed like the kind of thing that somebody special might be called.

Princess grew up very proud of her name, even though some of the other toads made fun of her for it. They liked to point out that she wasn't actually a princess, as if she needed to be told.

She hoped that one day she might actually become a real princess, and then all the toads who had laughed at her in the past would feel very silly. She knew this wasn't very likely as toads do not normally become princesses except in fairy stories, and this story has no fairies in it. Still, young girls like to dream, and Princess was a world-champion level dreamer—if only there was any dreaming competition to be champion of.

Because she was so fond of dreaming, Princess liked to imagine all the wonders that lay outside of her home. She spent her days exploring in order to discover new things to dream about. She explored the trees and fields around the pond where she lived, and she explored the rocks and pools over the nearby hill. She explored caves and valleys, and explored streams and rivers. She explored other places too but I think you get the general idea. Every day she got a little bit braver and wandered a little bit further from home.

There wasn't much else for a toad to do anyway, apart from sitting around croaking and eating bugs. Even if you're a very hungry toad, bugs are not particularly tasty. In fact, most of them are downright disgusting. If you've ever sucked on a beetle you'll already know this.

Chapter 1

Where the story actually starts

Our story starts on a day like any other. As usual, Princess got up early and had a quick breakfast of foul-tasting bugs, which were as disgusting as usual. She said goodbye to her parents before setting out to explore.

"Don't forget your lovely bug sandwiches!" her mother said. Not entirely by accident, Princess left without them and was soon hopping away through the tall grass.

The warm sun shone brightly as it rose in the blue sky. That's got nothing at all to do with the story, but it's the kind of thing that people write in books to make them longer. You probably already know that the sun is warm and the sky is blue. What actually matters is that Princess hopped and hopped, enjoying the feeling of being out exploring again, even though she did the same thing every day.

She climbed up a small hill that she had only climbed about a thousand times and hopped round a big rock. There she was surprised to meet a large red and blue-striped snake.

Most small animals would be scared to meet a snake face to face. Snakes have a nasty habit of eating small animals. It's not something they really want to do, as most snakes are very nice once you get to know them. But when you're a snake you tend to do snake-like things.

Princess wasn't scared at all, though. She knew that toads do not taste very nice (seriously, don't ever lick one) and she was sure that the snake wouldn't be interested in eating her. So, she hopped up to him and said brightly, "Good morning!"

"Is it?" grumbled the snake. He didn't look very happy at all, which is quite difficult for snakes as most of the time their faces don't move very much. "I don't think it's very good at all," he continued, "in fact, I think it's one of the worst days in the world, ever."

"Oh dear," replied Princess, "what on earth is the matter? Is there something I can do?"

"I doubt it. Unless you happen to have eight thousand socks with you."

At this point, the snake looked up hopefully. "Do you," he said, "have eight thousand socks?" He said this as if he expected to see Princess pull thousands of socks out of a pocket.

Like most toads, Princess didn't have any pockets, and definitely wasn't carrying any socks.

She wasn't even carrying her own socks, as toads don't tend to wear them. Toads may not always be the cleverest creatures, but even they know that socks get all wet when you jump in the water, and nobody likes wearing wet socks.

"I'm sorry," said Princess sadly, "I don't have any socks with me. I don't even own any socks. Why on earth do you need so many?"

"Well," said the snake sadly, "my name is Jim and I'm the First Grand Royal Sock-Finder General. It's a very special and important job, even though the King only created it last week. It's my job to find all the single socks that disappear in the wash."

"That sounds exciting!" replied Princess, not at all sure that finding socks could ever be exciting. "But has somebody really lost EIGHT THOUSAND socks?"

Jim looked up, "Oh yes—it sounds like a lot, doesn't it? But the King has a lot of socks."

The King really did have a lot of socks—he was a great fan of socks and liked to have a different pair for every day. Not just every day of the week, but every day of the year, and the next year, and the next. He would often wear one pair for breakfast and then by tea-time he might have changed them four or five times. His kingdom was mostly a peaceful place and there really wasn't much else for him to do anyway.

"Single socks have been disappearing for a long time, and the King doesn't have any pairs left," Jim continued. "So, he appointed a First Grand Royal Sock-Finder General—that's me—to find them. If I don't find at least some of the royal socks then I'll be in trouble. The King is very grumpy without his socks, and he'll probably throw me in the palace dungeon if I don't come back with them. I've been looking all week but haven't found a single one."

Princess looked around her. "But what on earth are you doing out here? Why would the socks be in the middle of nowhere? Shouldn't you be looking in the palace laundry?"

"Yes, I did think of that," said Jim, "but I assume that one of the laundry workers would have noticed eight thousand socks if they were in there. In fact, I don't think they're in any room in the palace at all. I've done some calculations and worked out that the only place you can hide eight thousand socks is somewhere big enough to hide eight thousand socks, which is probably outside— so here I am."

Jim sat up as high as he could by balancing on his tail, and he looked around. "Did you, by any chance, pass a pile of eight thousand socks on your way here?"

"I think I would have mentioned that by now," replied Princess, "but don't you worry. I'll help you find those socks as sure as my name is Princess Toad, which it is. I'm not actually a princess, though, in case you were wondering."

Princess still didn't think that finding socks was all that exciting, and spending the day with a grumpy snake wasn't really something she'd like to do either. But what did interest her was going to see the palace and the King. If there was a king then there might be a prince. And if there was a prince then she might meet him and they might fall head over heels in love and get married, and then she would be a real princess and—

"Stop thinking about marrying a prince," said Jim. "I can always tell when young girls start thinking about princes. Their eyes glaze over and they get this curious far-away look on their faces. You should know that Prince Glamchaps is probably too busy riding horses, trying on expensive clothes and eating fine food to fall in love with a toad. Princes don't usually tend to fall in love with toads, anyway."

"Well," replied Princess, "Prince Glamchaps hasn't met me yet. I'm sure he's just been waiting for the right toad to come along."

Jim was not convinced. "I very much doubt it," he said. "Anyway, I expect that he's only going to want to meet you if we find the King's socks. If we turn up at his door carrying all eight thousand of them I'm sure he'll be very grateful."

"Not to mention surprised," said Princess. "If we manage to carry eight thousand socks, I think anybody would be surprised."

Princess imagined laying thousands of socks grandly at the feet of Prince Glamchaps and receiving a royal kiss. It wasn't the kind of thing most toads imagined but, as you might have gathered from the story so far, Princess was not like most toads.

Chapter 2

This is the bit where they go to the palace

"I've done a lot of exploring," said Princess, "but I've never seen thousands of socks piled up anywhere, so there's no point looking round here." A small hill near to a pond really didn't seem like the best place to find lost socks. "I think the best thing would be to head to the palace and see if we can work out where the socks are going to in the first place."

"You really just want to go to the palace and meet the prince, don't you?" Jim sighed.

"Not at all!" replied Princess, who really just wanted to go to the palace and meet the prince.

Jim had been wandering around for a long time so he was ready to go back home for a while anyway. "All right," he said, "we'll go to the palace. Then you can try to find out where all the socks are disappearing from. If you help me to find them, I'll introduce you to the prince."

Jim had never actually met Prince Glamchaps in person. In fact, he'd never met any prince, despite living at the palace. And he definitely didn't have any idea about how a snake might introduce a toad to a prince. Still, getting somebody to help him find those socks was the most important thing at the moment—he'd work out how to do the introduction once the socks were safely back in their rightful home.

So, they both turned right at the rock and set off towards the palace, hopping and sliding through the grass, over twigs and pebbles in a direction that Princess had never been before.

"Isn't this exciting?" she cried.

"Not really," replied Jim.

Now I hope you haven't skipped ahead and read the title of the next chapter, because if you have then you'll know what's going to happen when they get to the palace. Or you might be able to guess, at least. So please don't read it yet.

You might really want to read the next chapter's title now, but there are only a few more pages to go until you get there. And if you do skip ahead, you'll miss reading about a King wearing nothing but his underpants. I don't know if that's a good thing or not, but turn the page to find out.

If you're still reading, you'll want to know that after a little while, Princess and Jim arrived at a huge palace. When I say it was huge, I really do mean it was absolutely massive, with turrets and flags and high walls and bright banners.

In a way, it's quite surprising that Princess had never seen it while exploring. Then again, she had always gone the same way around the big rock where she met Jim and had never turned right before.

"What an amazing palace!" cried Princess.

"Is it?" wondered Jim. It was the only palace he'd

ever seen so he didn't know if it was a particularly nice one or not.

Princess and Jim hopped and slid up the huge steps that led up to the main gates. Hop, slide, hop, slide, hop, slide, hop, slide, hop, slide, hop, slide—and so on. There were lots of steps and it took a long time to get to the top, which is quite lucky as it gives me a chance to work out what happens next in the story.

At the top of the steps stood the King, looking out across his kingdom wearing nothing but his underpants. I mean that the king was wearing the underpants—the kingdom wasn't wearing them. They probably wouldn't stretch that large anyway as the King's kingdom was a very big place.

Anyway, you don't normally find kings standing out in front of their palaces almost naked, but on this particular morning the King was having a bad day.

Yesterday he had received some new breakfast socks and was looking forward to wearing them whilst eating his toast and jam. But when he'd come to put them on this morning, the King could only find one sock. Being a breakfast sock, it had pictures of particularly royal-looking fried eggs on it, but on its own it was no use for somebody with two feet.

"Bother and bother!" the King had cried, and in his frustration, he had slammed his fist on the breakfast table, causing his toast to jump into the air. It flew gracefully through the air and landed on his best royal tracksuit. Flying toast always lands with the stickiest side downwards, so the King's clothes ended up covered with jam.

While taking off his sticky clothes, the King had tripped over an eggcup, which had also fallen onto the floor, and he banged his head on the table. The bump made a glass of orange juice tip over, which then poured onto his head while he was lying on the ground.

Not a very enjoyable breakfast at all and only slightly better than Friday's, when a vat of porridge had spilled down the chimney and flooded the breakfast room with the King in it.

The King was never in a very good mood anyway because of his missing socks, so this was too much for him to bear. He had stormed out of the palace in his underwear and was now looking around for somebody to shout at. Shouting at people is how kings make themselves feel better, as it reminds people how important they are.

"YOU! SNAKE!" he roared, seeing Jim and Princess finally reach the top of the steps. "I now have eight thousand AND ONE missing socks. You haven't found ANY of them, have you?"

"Umm, no," replied Jim nervously, "but I have found this toad who—"

"I SEE," interrupted the king, "so you have finally found THE CULPRIT—the SOCK STEALER. I might have known it would be a toad. Never trust a toad, that's what I always say."

The King had never actually said anything to anybody about toads, but that didn't seem to matter because he was so angry.

"Actually, no—" started Jim, but the King wasn't listening. He was too excited to finally have somebody to blame for his sock problem.

"GUARDS!" he shouted, "Arrest this toad at once and throw it in the dungeon. We'll find out where it's hidden those socks!" And with that, twenty royal guards came running out of the palace gates and they all attempted to arrest Princess at the same time.

If you've ever tried to pick up a toad, imagine trying to pick it up together with a friend. And

then imagine that another friend wants to join in, and then another, and then another sixteen friends. And this was a toad that really didn't want to be picked up. The result was that Princess went flying into the air and landed on the King's head. This did not go down well with the King.

"Assaulting the King! How dare you!" he cried, and a guard quickly grabbed Princess from the King's head and carried her into the palace, followed by nineteen other guards who were all trying to look like they were doing something useful.

Princess was so shocked that she didn't say anything at all as she was being carried away. All that Jim could do was stare, with his mouth open wide.

"Don't just stand there," commanded the King, "find out where that toad has hidden my socks. NOW!" And he shouted the last word so loudly that Jim jumped into the air and hurried into the palace behind the guards, still without saying anything. Snakes aren't usually very good at jumping, so you can tell how surprised he was.

He really didn't know what to do now. Even though it wasn't his fault, he felt very bad about getting Princess into so much trouble.

Chapter 3

*A dungeon is not a nice place
to spend a sunny day*

"This is why toads shouldn't go to palaces," said Jim. "They don't usually get invited anyway. Most royal people don't know many toads, and if they're going to kiss something that crawled out of a pond, they usually prefer frogs."

Jim had found the cell where Princess was locked up. It wasn't difficult to find because the twenty guards who had arrested her all felt that they wouldn't be doing their jobs unless they each took it in turns to check her chains and make sure the door was locked. Jim had arrived at the dungeon as the thirteenth guard was just checking the locks. Another seven were still waiting for their turn, so Jim had joined the back of the queue.

Now that all the guards had gone somewhere else in order to look busy and avoid doing any real work, Jim and Princess could talk.

"This visit to the palace," said Princess, "has not gone exactly like I expected. I don't really feel that I'm very much closer to finding any socks or getting a kiss from a prince."

She was sat in the middle of a dungeon cell that was far too big for her. The guards had attempted to put chains around her, but the palace dungeon was not designed for toads and they kept slipping off. In the end, the guards had just left the chains in a pile near to her and satisfied themselves that they were definitely locked.

"The King is never going to listen to either of us," Jim said. "Once he's made his mind up about something, he'll never change it. If he thinks you're to blame for stealing the socks, the only way we're ever going to get you free is to find the real thief."

"Yes," replied Princess, "but how are we going to do that when I'm stuck in this cell?"

"Don't you worry," said Jim, "we'll have you out of this cell in no time."

And with that, he reached up his tail and poked it into the lock of the cell door.

It's a bit difficult to work out which bit of a snake is its tail, as a snake is pretty much all tail with a face at one end. But Jim wiggled his rear end around in the lock for a while until there was a click. The cell door swung open and Princess hopped out into the corridor and brushed herself down.

"Thank you!" she exclaimed. "I was only in there for three and a half minutes but that was about four minutes too long for me. How did you do that thing with your tail?"

Jim waved the tip of his tail proudly. "Just a skill I picked up on my travels," he said. "It's very handy for times when you bring a toad to a palace and she gets locked up by a bad-tempered king."

"Does that happen often?" asked Princess.

"More often than it should do," said Jim thoughtfully.

Jim would have raised his eyebrows at this point, but he was a snake and he didn't have any to raise. "Let's go and find the sock thief," he said.

So, Princess and Jim headed down the corridor, sticking to the shadows. They didn't intend to stick to the shadows but somebody had spilled some very sticky jam a few years ago and it had never been cleaned up.

"Yuck, I feel all slimy," complained Princess, wiping jam off her feet.

"Yes, that could also be because you're a toad," Jim pointed out as they reached the main dungeon door and looked out across a courtyard.

People were doing their very best to look busy in case the King came wandering past, but luckily nobody was looking in Princess and Jim's direction.

"We'll need to start in the laundry," suggested Jim, and they both crept round the edge of the courtyard until they reached a sloping corridor with a door at the bottom. Bubbles were pouring out from the cracks in the door and as Princess and Jim approached, they could hear the sound of sloshing water and cranking machines.

Pushing open the door, Princess and Jim saw huge brass washing machines spinning, and clothes lines full of royal garments hanging from the ceiling.

Pelicans were picking up the washing in their beaks and moving it from place to place around the laundry. Pelicans make great laundry

staff as they can pick up lots of clothes at once, but they find doing the ironing very difficult as they don't have any arms.

"Look, there's the head pelican," pointed out Jim, waving the tip of his tail at a large bird wearing a gold sash. "We should ask her what's going on with the socks and if she's seen anything suspicious."

"Won't she tell the King that I've escaped?" asked Princess.

"Of course not," said Jim. "Only the King and his guards know that you were arrested in the first

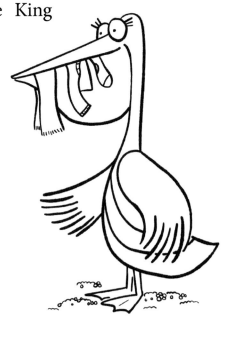

place. As long as we avoid any guards or kings, we should be fine."

So, Princess and Jim approached the head pelican and asked her about the King's socks. Her name was Maggie. You need to know that because I'm going to use her name in the next few lines and I don't want you thinking "Who on earth is Maggie?"

"Well, I don't know," said Maggie (see, I told you I was going to use her name). "I keep hearing about these missing socks but any pairs that come down here always end up leaving together. I even have an owl over there who keeps track of what comes and what goes out of this room."

She pointed towards a perch near the end of the room where a large barn owl sat with a clipboard under his wing. He was peering at baskets of clothes and nodding to himself as they went by.

In case you didn't know, owls are often used to keep track of numbers and do difficult sums. This isn't because they're any good at it but people think that owls are wise, and the feathers on their faces make them look as if they're wearing glasses. This makes them seem like they might be really quite clever, although most other birds are much more intelligent. Except, of course, for pigeons who are about as clever as two small rocks in a frying pan.

In fact, owls are terrible with numbers and most of them couldn't count to ten if you helped them with the first nine. What they're really good at is hiding this from everybody else.

This particular owl, Terry, kept a secret pet mouse under his wing to do all his sums for him. This worked out very well for Terry because mice are brilliant at maths, and they're also terrified of owls. Owls find mice very tasty to eat, although nobody knows why, least of all the mice.

So, the mouse did all of Terry's difficult sums, and Terry tried very hard not to eat her when he got hungry.

"Ah," said Terry, "you'll be wanting to ask me about shoes for snakes, won't you?"

He was trying very hard to sound wise and clever, but he really wasn't good at that kind of thing.

"Not at all," replied Jim. "We're interested in socks. Well, we're not actually 'interested' but we do need to find out where the missing ones are going to."

Terry frowned at Jim and Princess. "Socks, you say?" He reached down and pulled out his clipboard. "Let me just take a look."

Flipping through the paper on his board, he searched for the page listing the socks that had come and gone through the laundry. Although owls have excellent eyesight, they have trouble focusing on anything that isn't mouse-shaped. This makes reading very difficult for them and most owls never learn to read at all. This is why you've probably never seen an owl reading a book.

Terry's mouse reached out and chose the right page for him.

"Ah yes, here we are. Socks," Terry said, hoping that the mouse was correct. "The number of socks that came in last week was—"

"Four thousand six hundred and twenty," whispered the mouse.

"Four thousand six hundred and twenty," said Terry proudly, pretending that he was reading from the page. "And the number that went out was—"

"Four thousand six hundred and twenty," the mouse whispered again.

"Four thousand six hundred and twenty," repeated Terry. "They went out through that door."

Terry pointed to a large door in the corner of the room with a sign on it saying, "WASHED CLOTHES THIS WAY".

"Is that the same number?" he whispered to the mouse, trying to make it look like he was just mumbling thoughtfully to himself. Wise people often mumble thoughtfully as they think about important things, and Terry wanted very much to seem thoughtful.

"Yes, of course it is," hissed the mouse.

"Yes," whispered Terry, slightly embarrassed, "clearly I knew that." Terry had not known that at all.

"So that means no socks were lost here at all!" he said grandly to Jim and Princess.

Terry stood up and spread his wings dramatically, extremely proud that he had been able to give an answer to his visitors. But as he did this, he dropped his clipboard and the mouse onto the floor.

"Don't look at that!" cried Terry as he scooped up the mouse and the clipboard. He didn't want anybody to discover that he used a mouse for his work.

"That's just a snack. Yum!" he said, and he popped the mouse into his mouth. He smiled an embarrassed smile, his beak full. Princess and Jim looked at Terry and shook their heads.

"I think we need to follow the sock trail somewhere else," Princess suggested.

Jim agreed and they headed out of the laundry to find out where the washed clothes were taken to.

Once they had gone, Terry pulled the mouse out of his mouth by her tail.

"Sorry about that," he said, brushing her down and setting her back under his wing. The mouse did not look impressed.

"Let's not ever do that again," she said.

Chapter 4

The socks must be somewhere.
Unless they've been eaten

"Where *do* the socks go after they've been washed?" asked Princess.

"They go to be dried on the royal washing lines," Jim said. "I'm not sure where they are, but we just need to follow the signs."

The King had ordered helpful signs to be put up all over the palace a few years ago. Before then, nobody really knew where anything was as one of the King's hobbies was to expand his palace by building new towers, halls and rooms. He ordered something new to be built almost every week.

When he did, he tended to swap most of the old rooms around to make things easier to find. Of course, this didn't make anything easier to find at all, and made it very difficult for people to do their jobs.

One week you would be happily taking food from the kitchen into the breakfast room next door. The next week you would find that the kitchen had moved to a basement on the other side of the palace.

When you finally found the kitchen, you'd discover that the trays were stored in a new tray room at the top of a distant tower, and the ovens and taps didn't work because nobody had though to move the pipes.

Then you'd discover that the only way into the breakfast room was down a rope hanging through a hole in the ceiling because the King had built a new tooth-brushing room in front of the door.

At least by putting up signs everywhere, it was possible to simply move the signs around when any rooms changed. This should have been very easy but if a sign used to point left and it now needed to point right, the only solution was to hang it upside down. This was very helpful for sleeping bats but not much use for anybody else.

Anyway, while you were reading all that, Princess and Jim made their way into the palace gardens.

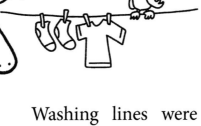

Washing lines were suspended from incredibly tall poles and brightly coloured clothes were being pegged onto the lines by giraffes. Teams of birds unpegged dry clothes and dropped them into baskets where beavers folded them neatly using their tails.

Hundreds of socks were lined up along one of the washing lines, and Jim and Princess could see immediately that they were all arranged in pairs.

"Well, at least we know that the socks are making it into the garden," said Princess.

"But we're no closer to find out where they're going to," grumbled Jim. "It's been like this ever since I was given my job. Nobody seems to know anything."

"Let's keep following the trail, though," suggested Princess, and she hopped over to where the beavers had just finished neatly folding and pressing thirty or forty pairs of socks.

"Do these socks all belong to the King?" Princess asked the nearest beaver.

"Yes, of course," he replied, slightly surprised. "All the socks in the palace belong to the King"

When the King's socks began to disappear, he had issued a royal decree that all socks were now the property of the crown. The King didn't want anybody else wearing socks if he couldn't have any.

Because of that, nobody else dared to wear socks at all any more.

"We used to all have such lovely socks," continued the beaver, "but you'd be busy doing your job and the King would come along and take whatever you were wearing. He would point out that your teddy-bear patterned actually socks belonged to him and you'd never see them again."

"Well," said Princess, "that's not very nice of him. I'm not sure I want to find his socks for him now."

"Remember that the King will lock you up again if he catches you," pointed out Jim, "at least until he gets his socks back. Maybe when the King's socks are returned, everybody else can start wearing their own again. Although I don't know why they would want to."

Snakes don't tend to wear socks as they don't have many feet to put them on. Snakes who *do* have feet probably aren't snakes at all—just incredibly confused lizards.

"I don't really know either," said Princess, "but let's find out what happens to these socks once they've been dried and folded."

They didn't have to wait long to find out, as the sock basket was picked up by a goat with extremely curly horns.

She hooked one horn through the handle and trotted off towards the palace with the basket hanging from the side of her head at a very odd angle.

"That doesn't look very safe," pointed out Princess.

"It's the only way to stop a goat from eating all the clothes before she gets to where she's going" replied Jim.

If you have a goat and want to use it to carry your washing, just make sure the basket goes nowhere near her mouth. It's quite easy for a goat to pick up a basket with her teeth but, more often than not, half the basket will be missing within a few minutes. You'll also find that your best pants are full of holes shaped suspiciously like goats' teeth.

If you're thinking of asking a goat to do your laundry, I suggest you choose another animal or maybe even do it yourself—it's a lot easier and your parents will thank you for it.

Princess and Jim followed the goat into the palace and up several flights of steps. Goats are very good at climbing steps and they do it very quickly, so Princess and Jim were completely exhausted by the time they reached the top.

They had already climbed the main palace steps earlier and toads and snakes don't tend to come across steps much in their normal daily lives. This means that they don't really get much practice at it. That's unless they happen to live in a Toad Tower full of nothing but small rooms and hundreds of flights of stairs. That's extremely unlikely, though, because it's something that I just made up.

Anyway, at the top of the steps the goat took the basket into a large bedroom filled with golden furniture and a giant bed covered with velvet blankets.

"This must be the King's bedroom!" exclaimed Princess, very excited to see where a king might sleep.

"Yes, indeed it is," agreed Jim. "Just make sure that he's not around anywhere. If he sees you, it's back to the dungeons for both of us!"

So, Princess and Jim crept around the edge of the room as the goat carried the basket into the King's dressing room.

The dressing room was lined on all sides with hundreds of almost identical drawers. The only way to tell one drawer apart from another was a small handwritten sign on the front of each, which said what was inside. This would have been much more helpful if every single sign didn't say "Socks" on it.

The goat began to unload the socks into one of the drawers by tipping her head until the socks poured out of the basket. This wasn't a particularly neat way to put socks into a drawer but as Princess and Jim watched they saw a pair of mice run out from a tiny door in the skirting board. The mice leapt up into the drawer and started to organise the socks neatly into rows, sorted by colour, texture and length.

Mice are not only good with numbers, but they love order and are ideal for sorting socks neatly. If you have a mouse living in your sock drawer, you'll know what I mean. That's unless you happen to have one

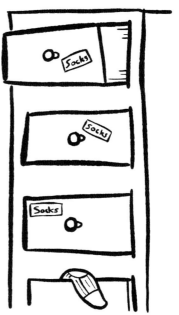

of those rare messy ones who chews up the socks, makes a nest and uses the corner as a toilet.

Once the goat and the mice had gone, Princess and Jim took a look inside the drawer.

"All socks present and correct," Jim said. "Socks never seem to disappear at all, right up until the moment that they do."

"And when's that?" Princess asked.

"I wish I knew," replied Jim. "But they always disappear in the end."

"Why don't we just watch this sock drawer and see what happens?" suggested Princess. "If we watch it all night and the socks are still there in the morning, then at least the King will have some socks tomorrow. And if they disappear then we'll see who takes them. Either way it's better than just giving up. Why didn't you watch the socks in their drawers before?"

"Because that's the most boring thing that anybody could think of doing," replied Jim. "Have you ever tried to watch a piece of furniture all night?"

"Not yet," said Princess. "But let's give it a go and see what happens!"

So, Princess and Jim found a hiding place behind a nearby curtain and settled down on a large vase to keep watch.

There were no flowers in the vase, so you might wonder why it was in the King's  dressing room at all. However, that's the kind of thing that you find in palaces because empty vases and other pointless ornaments take up lots of space. Kings and queens collect this kind of thing in order to pretend that they really do need lots and lots of rooms.

Anyway, if you've ever tried to watch a piece of furniture all night, you will know just how incredibly boring it is. Not just boring like "I can't think of anything to do" or "This TV program isn't very interesting" but the kind of boring where every part of your body wants to run around the room screaming in frustration. It's the kind of boring where you'd much rather be doing your maths homework or cleaning every toilet in the house rather than sitting still any longer.

Princess and Jim quickly got very bored indeed. They would both have fallen asleep within a few minutes if they hadn't kept prodding each other to stay awake. The worst thing was that it was barely

past tea-time and only just beginning to get dark. They still had the whole night to go.

"I expect that somebody has noticed you've escaped by now," Jim pointed out. "That means we're really going to have to do our best to stay hidden, as the guards are probably looking for us as we speak."

Princess's escape from the dungeon had indeed been noticed. When the dungeon-keeper had arrived to serve a healthy meal of cold cabbage and three-week old custard, he had found an empty cell. When the King had been told, he commanded fifty guards to search the palace from top to bottom until Princess was found.

This sounds like it would be plenty of guards to find somebody, but in fact it meant that nothing at all got done. Every single guard thought to himself, "Why do I need to do any searching? There are another forty-nine guards out there looking for just one toad, and surely that's enough. One more guard won't make much of a difference, so I might as well just have a nice cup of tea."

The result was that fifty guards took themselves off to different parts of the palace and each enjoyed a nice quiet cup of tea and a slice of cake. Princess wasn't in any danger of being found, although she had no way of knowing this.

As the sun set it began to get dark, and soon it was night time. You probably already know how the whole 'getting dark at night-time' thing works, but I thought I'd mention it just in case.

The dressing room's only light came from a single candle. This was lit at about half past seven by a pigeon who flew into the room with a box of matches, and then struggled for about twenty minutes trying to work out how to light the match.

It turned out that he had the match upside down and the box backwards, and every time he changed one thing, the other was still wrong. Pigeons, as I mentioned before, really are not very clever.

Princess and Jim stayed hidden the whole time and kept watching the sock drawer for minute after minute, hour after hour. They heard the palace clock strike eight, nine, ten, eleven and then twelve midnight.

Just as they were about to give up, there was a rattling sound and a metal grate covering a hole in the wall popped off and fell onto the floor. Into the room, carrying a small silver lantern, stepped a sock gnome.

Chapter 5

Yes, it's a Sock Gnome

Sock Gnomes are rarely seen in the open, but they're not at all rare or unusual. You've probably had several visit your house over the last few months, particularly if you have a washing machine.

Long ago, in the olden days, people used to wash socks by hand (ask your parents about it—they'll be thrilled) and they never let the socks out of their sight. This made it very hard for Sock Gnomes to do their very important job. As I'm sure you know, this is to steal single socks so that nobody has a complete pair.

Usually the only pairs left in your drawer are those that have holes in them.

Since people started getting lazy and using washing machines, though, Sock Gnomes have had a much easier task. Now they just climb into the machine when nobody is looking and take whatever socks they like the look of.

Sometimes they even get brave and steal underpants, pull buttons from shirts or sprinkle dark fluff all over light-coloured clothes. Nobody has ever discovered where they get the fluff from.

It's important that you don't confuse Sock Gnomes with Sock Elves (who knit socks for people who really don't need them) or Sock Trolls (who we'll get to in a bit). Sock Gnomes wear brightly-coloured hats, large boots and fake beards.

It's a well-known fact that gnomes can't grow beards so they have to make do with beards made from cat hair or hedgehog spines. The gnomes with hedgehog-spine beards tend not to be popular at parties, as they usually end up bursting all the balloons.

Anyway, the Sock Gnome who crept into the King's dressing room was dressed in purple and green and he was called Eric. It doesn't really matter what his name was as I'm not going to use it again, but that was his name and he liked it.

He crept over to the drawers and sniffed with his large gnome nose, seeking out the particular scent that comes only from socks in pairs. With a grunt, he climbed up to the fourteenth drawer on the left, six rows up, which was unsurprisingly labelled "Socks". This was the drawer that Princess and

Jim were watching, and they stared in amazement as the Sock Gnome pulled open the drawer and peered inside.

He began to separate pairs and pull single socks out of the drawer. They all went into his large sock sack as Princess turned to Jim and whispered.

"Should we stop him? I wonder if we should catch him and ask him where he's taking those socks."

"No," hissed Jim, "that would be a terrible idea. Sock Gnomes are very convincing liars. If we asked him where he lived he would soon have us believing that he had a house on the moon and that his grandmother was made of lettuce."

"So, what do we do?" asked Princess.

"Wait for him to leave and then follow him," Jim suggested.

It would certainly be easier than attempting to catch a Sock Gnome anyway. This is so hard that every year in Sweden they hold a grand gnome-catching contest with huge prizes and golden trophies. Nobody ever actually catches any gnomes, though, and almost everybody gets badly hurt in the attempt. It's a mystery why they even try in the first place.

So, Princess and Jim sat very quietly while the Sock Gnome filled his sack and gently closed the drawer, being careful not to make a noise and wake the King next door.

Princess and Jim hadn't even thought about the King being in the bedroom next door. If they had, they might have been a lot more nervous and a lot less bored.

Still, once the gnome had finished, he climbed down to the floor and back through the metal grate in the wall, closing it softly behind him. Princess and Jim crept from their hiding place and rushed over to the grate. They could see the light from the gnome's lantern gradually disappearing down the tunnel, which led through the walls and out of the palace.

"Help me, quickly!" whispered Jim, tugging at the grate with his tail. Princess grabbed hold of the bars and pulled, moving the whole thing up enough for the two of them to squeeze through.

They headed down the tunnel as fast as they could, following the sound of the Sock Gnome's footsteps and the lamp-light disappearing into the distance.

They soon reached the end of the tunnel and blinked in the moonlight. It was a full moon and the palace gardens were lit up as brightly as the middle of the night can be. This isn't usually very much, but it's enough to see where your feet are.

The Sock Gnome was heading across the grass towards a gap in the wall. It was just about big enough for a gnome to fit through. I should probably mention that Sock Gnomes are slightly bigger than a squirrel but not as large as a cat.

Telling you this earlier might have made the gnome easier to imagine, but there were a couple of pictures to help you. If somebody

is reading this book to you and isn't showing you the pictures, you'll just have to make up what the gnome looked like. I'm sure you can picture him squeezing through the hole with Princess and Jim not far behind.

Princess and Jim passed through the hole easily, and once they were on the other side they found themselves in a dense forest with thick brambles covering the ground. The gnome had cut a tunnel through the brambles which allowed him to travel easily without getting scratched. This made the brambles very disappointed.

Brambles have one purpose in life, and that is to scratch people as much as possible. The only reason most of them produce any fruit at all is to get you nice and close with the promise of juicy blackberries or raspberries. Once you're within reach of a bramble, it attaches its thorns to as many of your clothes as it can. It won't let go until you're completely fed up and have gone off fruit for life. Nobody knows why it does this.

Anyway, as Princess and Jim followed the gnome through the forest, the brambles began to thin out and soon disappeared completely.

Instead the forest floor began to be covered with toadstools. At first the toadstools were dull brown things, looking like mushrooms who were trying a bit too hard, but as they walked on, the toadstools became bigger and bigger, brighter and brighter. Blue, red, yellow and purple toadstools appeared in ever-increasing sizes, and soon they were towering above Princess and Jim as big as small trees.

The Sock Gnome kept going. He knew exactly where he was heading and he threaded his way through the toadstools at great speed.

"Look," hissed Jim, "lights!" And, sure enough the toadstools ahead were lit up by hanging lanterns of all colours, and the largest toadstools even had windows in them, shining brightly by the candlelight inside.

Princess and Jim crept around one of the largest toadstools, making sure to stay out of sight. They stopped as they came to a wide clearing. The largest homes were arranged in a circle around one huge toadstool.

This toadstool was orange with white spots and its sides were filled with windows which were lighting up the night. Through the windows Jim and Princess could hear the sounds of many Sock Gnomes laughing and joking. The Sock Gnome that they were following went through the biggest door and at once there was a loud cheer from inside.

"What on earth is going on?" asked Princess. "I thought that Sock Gnomes just stole socks in order to cause trouble. This seems like they're actually doing something with them."

"Yes," said Jim, "it does seem like that. Let's get closer and find out what they're using them for." And he slithered over to a window and peered inside. "Come and see!" he hissed.

Princess hopped over to Jim and looked through the window at what was happening in the toadstool. It was completely hollowed out and inside there was one huge hall. In the middle was an enormous pile of roughly eight thousand

and twenty-six socks, all stitched together in a very confusing pattern. Ropes had been threaded through some of the stitching and one end was hanging from large hooks in the far wall.

Surrounding the pile of socks were hundreds of Sock Gnomes, furiously sewing, and Princess could see that the gnome who had just arrived was emptying his sack onto a large table by the door. Several gnomes rushed up and each grabbed a sock, taking it over to a part of the sock pile where there was a hole.

After two or three minutes, a particularly old gnome with a walking stick and a long purple

cloak climbed to the top of the pile and cleared his throat.

"Ahem!" he coughed, and then "Ahem!" again when he noticed that none of the other gnomes were paying any attention to him.

"A-H-E-M!" he coughed so loudly that if you'd been there you might have been worried he was about to explode. The Sock Gnomes all around the room fell silent and stopped what they were doing.

"The Grand Sock Bridge is almost complete!" announced the old gnome. "Tonight, we shall stitch the final socks in place and our bridge will be finished. We will finally be able to cross the gap and join our sock brothers and sisters on the other side!"

A huge cheer went up around the room and there was a lot of clapping. The gnomes who were stitching the last few socks into place finished their jobs and stood up proudly, and then every gnome in the hall lifted up whichever part of the sock pile was closest to them.

"That," said Jim, "is one of the weirdest things I've ever seen, and I've seen some pretty weird things."

Princess nodded, "It is pretty odd, but at least we've found the King's socks. Now what do we do? We can't just walk in there and ask for the socks back, and I think they'd notice if we tried to take them."

Jim looked worried. "Exactly," he said. "I really don't have a clue what to do next."

Chapter 6

What to do with several thousand socks

The Sock Gnome village was built, or rather grown—you don't tend to build toadstools— in the forest next to a deep gorge. If you're not sure what a gorge is, imagine that you were very small and you lived on a biscuit. Yes, I know that's a bit strange. But now imagine that somebody broke the biscuit in half and pulled the two pieces apart so that there was a crack running all the way through it. That gap in the middle would be like a gorge and if you were really, really small you'd have a hard time getting across it. Quite why you were living on a biscuit and who broke it in half is not something you should worry too much about.

In the case of the Sock Gnomes, the gorge wasn't biscuit-sized at all, but was incredibly deep and about as far across as two buses laid end to end. If you threw a stone (or a bus) into it, it would take a long time before you heard it hit the bottom, and nobody had ever actually been down there. Well, not deliberately at least. On the other side of the gap there was another village, also made of toadstools, where the Sock Trolls lived.

Remember when I said earlier that you shouldn't confuse Sock Gnomes with Sock Trolls? Well, the only difference between the two is that Sock Gnomes wear pointy hats and fake beards, while Sock Trolls think that hats are pointless and beards are silly—so they don't wear either of them. As a result, Sock Trolls are much happier because they don't spend a lot of their time worrying about what colour hat to wear or whether or not their beard is going to get them invited to parties.

Long ago, back when sliced bread was the latest cool thing, the Sock Gnomes and Sock Trolls were exactly the same as each other and they lived together in one big village. They were very happy and they used to knit their own socks instead of stealing them.

Then one day the ground shook violently and the village was split in two, dividing the terrified gnomes and trolls with a gap that they couldn't cross.

The earthquake that caused the gap wasn't natural, but was actually the result of the King's great-great-great-great grandfather moving his table tennis room to be closer to the chocolate-coating chamber. If you've never tried playing table tennis with a chocolate-coated ball, then you're probably not a king. Or maybe you are, but you have far more important things to do.

From that day forwards the Gnomes and Trolls lived separately, never able to meet up with each other for a friendly cup of tea, or get together to knit new socks.

Over time, the Gnomes forgot how to knit and ended up stealing socks one at a time, and the Trolls gave up wearing socks at all. Instead, they learned to bake wonderful cakes, which annoyed the Gnomes immensely as they could smell them from the other side of the gorge but could never taste them.

But that's enough about gnome and troll history—I seem to remember that I was telling you a story about a toad and a snake, so let's get back to that.

Princess and Jim watched through the window as the Sock Gnomes rolled the socks up into an enormous tube and then discovered that it wouldn't fit through the door. They continued to watch as the gnomes unrolled their construction and finally dragged it outside by stretching it out and heaving at one end.

"Is that really a bridge?" said Jim.
"Well, it's definitely long—but why would anybody build a bridge out of socks?" replied Princess.

The gnomes carried the socks to the edge of the deep gorge, and Jim and Princess followed at a distance. They weren't too worried about being seen, as all the gnomes were looking the other way. As they watched, two gnomes picked up the ropes that were sewn into the socks and they tied them onto arrows. Then they pulled out bows that were nearly twice as tall as they were and aimed them at the Sock Troll village.

"Fire!" shouted the old gnome, and the two arrows were launched off into the darkness, trailing the ropes behind them. Remember that it was still night time—Sock Gnomes are not very patient at the best of times and nobody had even thought about waiting until the morning.

Instead of falling down into the gorge, the ropes stayed tight as if somebody had grabbed hold of them at the other side. In fact, several somebodies had grabbed hold of the ropes and were now pulling with all their might, as the ropes started to drag the socks across the gap.

As the socks started to move, a bunch of very enthusiastic gnomes tied the ropes onto large wooden poles that had already been dug into the ground at the edge of the gorge. They tied the closest socks onto a pair of wooden boards that looked as though they were likely to fall into the

gap at any moment, but everything held together firmly.

"Well, that's definitely a bridge," Princess said as the socks flattened out under the ropes and the shape became clearer.

Eventually the socks stopped moving, as they now spread from one side of the gorge to the other, forming a slightly wobbly, but very colourful, bridge. A single gnome ran forwards and stepped carefully onto the socks. They didn't fall apart and the bridge didn't break, so she took several more steps until she was almost lost in the darkness.

"It works!" she shouted happily, and started jumping up and down on the bridge.

"Well done everybody!" cried the old gnome. "Our bridge is complete and we can re-join our brothers and sisters across the gap. This is a happy day! Or night, even." All the gnomes cheered, clapped and hugged each other.

"Finally, we can share our love of hats and beards with the Sock Trolls, and hopefully they will share some of their cakes with us. But that can wait until tomorrow. For now," he cried, "it's bedtime!"

And all the gnomes immediately turned around to head off to their individual toadstools.

"Hello," said Jim, as he and Princess stood face to face with several hundred slightly confused Sock Gnomes.

Chapter 7

There's a lot of talking in this chapter

"And who," said the old gnome, "are you? How did you find our village? Where did you come from? What are you doing?"

Princess and Jim didn't know what to say, mostly because they didn't know which question to answer first.

"I'm Princess, and this is Jim," said Princess eventually. "We followed a gnome from the palace, where he stole some socks from the King. It seems that you gnomes have stolen quite a lot of socks, actually."

"We were trying to find out where the all the socks had gone," added Jim. "If we don't return them then the King will throw us in his dungeon."

The old gnome looked confused. "Why would the King throw a princess into the dungeon?" he asked. "That doesn't seem very like a king-like thing to do."

"I'm not actually a princess," said Princess, "that's just my name."

"Well, that's just silly," replied the old gnome, "and whoever heard of a toad with a name?"

He looked at Jim and Princess, still confused. "Why would a toad and a snake be looking for the King's socks?"

"It's my job," said Jim, "but I think Princess is doing it so that she can marry a prince."

Princess felt a bit embarrassed but knew it was true. She decided not to say anything.

"Hah! That's even more silly than your name," said the old gnome. "You'd better come with me, I think," and he started to walk over to a very grand-looking toadstool on the edge of the clearing.

"I think we should follow," said Jim, looking around him at all the Sock Gnomes who still staring at them.

The old gnome led Princess and Jim into his toadstool and waved his hand to suggest that they sit down. They took a seat on some smaller toadstools that were obviously meant to be used as chairs, and they waited while the old gnome put the kettle on to boil.

"Can't do much talking without a nice cup of tea," said the old gnome. "Hopefully we'll soon be able to have a nice slice of cake to go with it, now that we've built our bridge."

"You could have crossed the bridge and got some cake by now," suggested Jim.

"Heavens, no," cried the old gnome, "it's far too late for that. We already forgot to have supper because we were working too hard."

He pottered about the kitchen, fetching the toadstool tea and finding three cups.

"Now it's bedtime but I can probably spend a few minutes talking to you before I settle down," he said. "I just need to decide whether to let you go or to throw you into the gorge—nothing too important."

"It's quite important to us," said Princess.

Once the kettle had boiled, the old gnome poured out cups of tea for each of them. Snakes don't usually drink tea because they find it very hard to hold the cup, but Jim tried his best to balance it on his tail without spilling any.

The old gnome sat down in an armchair which looked like it was made out of old leaves and twigs.

"It's made of old leaves and twigs," said the old gnome, stroking the chair. "Isn't it lovely?

"But how rude of me," he gasped, "I haven't even introduced myself. My name is Sebastian

Grunglenubs and I am the Great Grand Gnome, or GGG. Everybody calls me Gee for short."

"Hello Gee," said Princess and Jim together.

"I must admit I'm confused, though," said Gee. "What on earth makes you think that we would give you all our socks? It's taken a long time to collect them, and we now have a very nice bridge."

"Those socks don't belong to you," Jim pointed out. "They belong to the King and to all the people of the kingdom. He's now a very grumpy king as he doesn't have any socks to wear."

"That's not true! Not true at all!" exclaimed Gee, raising a finger. "The King still has well over eight thousand socks. We've only taken one of each sock, so that leaves the King with enough socks to make over four thousand pairs. If he won't wear them because they don't match then he shouldn't be so fussy!"

"That's a good point," said Princess, "but I hear that people like to wear matching socks, although I don't know why. The King definitely likes matching pairs and he'll keep looking for me until he gets them back."

Gee looked concerned. "Is he looking for you now?" he asked.

"Probably," Princess said. "I wouldn't be surprised if he's got his royal guards searching the entire forest right now."

At this point in the story, it's worth pointing out that it's still night-time. I know I haven't been telling you the time regularly as we've gone along, but for Princess and Jim it was about half past three in the morning.

That's the kind of 'morning' that isn't really morning at all. It's still dark and very few people are awake. The only people who are up are those who have to go to work very early, or people who were too scared to go to bed in the first place because there was a spider in their bedroom.

So, the King was still fast asleep and all his guards were comfortably tucked up in their beds, full of tea and cake. They might search the forest in the morning, but you'll have to keep reading to find out.

"Well, that's not good," said Gee, thoughtfully. "I could do without palace guards stomping all over our toadstools and causing trouble. But you can't have our bridge. We've waited years to get back together with the Sock Trolls and to try their cake. Let's sleep on it and we'll see if we can find an answer in the morning."

And with that, he got up, blew the candles out and went upstairs to bed. Most toadstools have a bedroom upstairs, and it's generally a lot larger than the downstairs if you think about the shape of a toadstool. However, the ceilings are often very low, so it's only useful for lying down.

Princess and Jim sat there in the dark, looking at each other. Or at least they looked in each other's general direction, as they now couldn't see anything.

"So, what now?" asked Jim. "We could just leave, although I'm not sure where we would go. If we go back to the palace, we'll end up in the dungeon."

"But if we stay here," said Princess, "there's a chance that we might get thrown down a big hole in the ground."

"Or we might get the socks and some cake," suggested Jim.

"That's true," agreed Princess.

So, Princess and Jim decided to stay until morning and soon fell asleep on the toadstool chairs. They had not been designed for sleeping on, so it was almost impossible to get comfortable. Princess and Jim spent the whole night tossing, turning and repeatedly falling onto the floor.

When morning came, Gee appeared and found Princess and Jim sitting where he'd left them. He looked quite surprised.

"Did you think we would run away?" asked Princess, proud that they'd decided to stay.

"No," Gee frowned, "I just thought you might have found it a bit more comfortable on those beds. Toadstool chairs are not made for sleeping on," and he pointed towards two feather-lined beds in the corner of the room.

"Oh," said Jim.

"No matter," Gee continued, "grab one of those breakfast toadstools and we'll go and see the bridge." He took a small leaf-wrapped toadstool from the table and headed out of the door.

You might have noticed by now that toadstools feature a lot in the lives of gnomes. Gnomes sit on them, live in them, put things on them, burn them, paint them and eat them. Sometimes they'll do all those things to the same toadstool. This is only a good thing if you're a gnome. To everybody else they're annoying when they grow in the middle of your lawn and you could be extremely sick if you eat one. Jim and Princess wisely decided to leave the toadstool snacks to the gnomes and headed outside with Gee.

Although it was early, the bridge was already being used by lots of Sock Gnomes, and Jim and Princess saw their first Sock Trolls. Gnomes and trolls were chatting everywhere they looked, catching up on several generations of family history and finding out about things like Aunt Mabel's surprise marriage to a magpie, or cousin Henry's invention for gluing beards onto rabbits.

Gee led Princess and Jim across the bridge. It was much more solid than it looked, and it also felt very soft, like a posh carpet. In the light of day, you could see the patterns that the gnomes had woven together out of the socks. Blues and greens were mixed with reds and purples, and the whole thing looked like it could be the start of a promising career for a young fashion designer.

"We used socks," explained Gee, "because the King seemed to have an awful lot of spares that he wasn't using. How can anybody wear eight thousand pairs of socks at once? Even a centipede could get by for at least six months before he would have to do any washing."

"That kind of makes sense," said Jim, "but it's still stealing."

"Not to a Sock Gnome," Gee responded. "We don't steal socks, we just borrow them and then forget to return them. We have terrible memories."

"I don't think that's a very good excuse," said Princess.

At the other side of the bridge they were met by an old troll wearing purple robes just like Gee.

"Greetings!" cried the troll. "I am Frederick Trumblenubs and I am the Terribly Terrific Troll, or TTT. People call me Tee for short. Would you like a piece of cake?"

Princess, Jim and Gee followed Tee into a large toadstool that looked almost exactly like Gee's on the other side of the bridge. The toadstool was filled with the smell of cake, which would have been delicious if it hadn't been made out of toadstools.

"We have so much to discuss," began Gee, "but first there's the small matter of the King."

"Oh yes?" queried Tee. "What about him? I haven't come across a king in years. Are they still just as bad-tempered as ever?"

"I gather that they are," Gee said. "I'm afraid that this one is looking for his socks, and for these creatures here." Gee pointed to Princess and Jim. "If they don't return with his socks then the palace guards will come trampling all over our village and we'll never hear the end of it."

Tee looked confused. "So just tell the toad and the snake to give the socks back," he said.

"Well, actually," said Gee, "it's us gnomes who have got the socks."

"Oh dear, that does sound like a pickle," said Tee, cutting slices of cake. "I think you should probably just give the socks back and be done with it. It doesn't sound like it's worth the trouble to keep them. The trolls can always knit you a couple more pairs if your feet are cold."

"I don't think that will work," Gee said.

"Why ever not?"

"Because we used the socks to build the bridge," admitted Gee.

"You did?" Tee looked surprised, "I did think it had a lovely sock-like design. Well, well, well."

"If you can knit socks," said Princess, "why didn't you just knit your own bridge in the first place? Assuming that wool is a good thing to use to make a bridge, which I'm not at all sure about."

"Because," said Gee sharply, "only the Sock Trolls know how to knit."

"And only the Sock Gnomes know how to spin wool," added Tee. "It seems that if we give the King his socks back, we'll have no bridge. No bridge means no knitting."

"And no knitting means no bridge," said Gee.

Jim and Princess thought for a long time while Gee and Tee tucked into their toadstool cake. Finally, Princess spoke up.

"What if," she said, "we found you a replacement bridge? Would you be happy to give the King his socks back then?"

"Oh yes," said Gee, "to be honest, I'm sick of socks. It's all fun when you've been causing a bit of mischief by borrowing the odd sock here and there, but when you're taking thousands of socks and spending every night and day stitching them together, you soon get bored. I'd be glad to see the back of them as long as we can still have a bridge."

"Right then," said Jim, "that's settled then. We'll find you a new bridge and you can return the socks. Wonderful."

With that, Princess and Jim said their goodbyes and headed back across the bridge.

"I've just had a troubling thought," said Princess. "How on earth are we going to find a new bridge for the gnomes and trolls?"

"I have absolutely no idea," said Jim.

Chapter 8

Something might actually happen in this chapter

If you've got this far after all that talking, you're doing very well and you should give yourself a pat on the back. Or at least get as close as you can. It's difficult to pat yourself on the back without twisting your arm into a very awkward position. If somebody else patted you on the back like that you'd wonder what on earth they were doing.

Still, a lot more is going to happen in this chapter. The princess still has to escape her wicked stepmother and find all those dwarves to live with. Or that might be a different book. I assume that you'll find out if you keep reading.

"I think we should just tell the truth to the King," said Princess as she hopped along next to Jim. They were heading through the toadstools and back to the palace, hoping that they could find

somebody who could help them to build a new bridge.

"I think we should just go straight to the King and tell him exactly what has happened. He might help us to build the bridge."

"I don't think that's a good idea," Jim said. "The King won't change his mind. He'll still think it's all your fault and throw you back into the dungeon. And now," he sighed, "he'll be blaming me too."

Princess and Jim wondered who could help them to build a new bridge. It wasn't something that they had ever had to think about before, so they weren't sure how to work it out.

They were thinking so hard that they didn't notice the horse until it was almost on top of them. It's lucky that it was only 'almost' because if the horse really was on top of them, that would probably be the end of the story right here and now.

"Woah!" cried Prince Glamchaps from high up on his horse. "Steady there, Fluffkins. What have we here? Is this the escaped toad and her devious accomplice? I think it is!" And he drew his sword, and pointed it at Princess and Jim.

"Fluffkins? Who would call a horse Fluffkins?" asked Princess.

"I think we have other things to worry about," said Jim, looking at Princess with a glare.

"Well, I think it's a nice name," said Fluffkins, looking a little hurt.

"Steady on!" said the Prince. "You're the ones that everybody's been looking for." He sat up proudly. "So, I have apprehended the sock stealer, and the snake who helped her to escape. I also found some money behind the sofa and got an early birthday card from my auntie this morning, so this is turning out to be a very good day indeed."

"No!" cried Princess. "That's not true at all. It's nothing like that."

"Yes, it is," said the Prince angrily, "I definitely did get a card from my auntie this morning."

"She means about the socks," corrected Jim. "She didn't steal them."

"Ah," smiled the Prince, "but of course she did. She's a toad, and we all know what toads do with socks."

Of course, he didn't actually know what toads did with socks, because toads didn't normally have socks (see page 8). If a toad did have a sock, he probably wouldn't know what to do with it. He would probably end up using it to keep bugs in, as this does make bugs slightly tastier. Instead of being completely disgusting, they become simply very horrible indeed.

No toad in the history of toad-kind had ever stolen any socks at all, but the prince wasn't going to be put off by a little thing like the truth. Not if it got in the way of a good story. And this was one story he was looking forward to telling his father, the King.

"You're coming with me. Quick march to the palace!" commanded the Prince.

"That's where we were going anyway," complained Princess. "Can you give us a lift?"

"What? On Fluffkins?" The Prince looked dismayed. "Of course not. Royal people do not share their horses with common toads or snakes."

Princess began to think that the chances of a real romance between the Prince and her were slipping away very quickly.

She said, "We need to make a replacement bridge for the Sock Gnomes and the Sock Trolls, and then we can get the King's socks back."

"I have never heard anything so ridiculous in my whole life!" the Prince lied.

Of course, he had heard many ridiculous things—just this morning his left shoelace assistant had tried to convince him that she was the second cousin to the Grand Duke of Nozbury. The Prince thought that this was highly unlikely, as his shoelace assistant lived in a pig sty and ate mostly muddy potatoes.

The Prince wouldn't listen to anything else that Princess or Jim tried to tell him. Instead he ended up having a wonderfully interesting conversation about turnips with his horse while they walked towards the palace.

"This is not looking good," grumbled Jim.

"No," agreed Princess, "it doesn't look like I'll be marrying the Prince any time soon, or even getting an affectionate hug."

"I meant about being thrown into a dungeon," Jim said.

"Oh yes, that too."

Eventually they arrived back at the palace. It seemed to take a lot longer to get back than it had to get out in the first place, but neither the Prince nor Fluffkins were looking where they were going, and they ended up walking around in circles for nearly half an hour. Princess and Jim trudged behind, feeling like the day just could not get any worse, and with aching backs from sleeping on toadstools too.

It might be surprising to learn that snakes can get bad backs if they sleep in the wrong position—after all, they seem to be able to curl themselves around almost anything. But a bed has to be just right for them to be comfortable, which is why you've probably never seen a snake sleeping on a cheap mattress.

The King met them when they arrived. He had seen the Prince going round and round the palace gardens for the last half an hour and thought he might find out what was going on.

"Ah hah!" he cried, seeing Princess and Jim. "You've caught that devious toad and her slithering companion. Well, toad—are you ready to tell me where you have hidden my socks?"

"I haven't hidden them anywhere, but I know where they are," she began.

"I knew it!" The King slammed his fist down on a decorative border, which caused several plant pots to fall off and break. "So, where are they?"

Princess tried to explain about the Sock Gnomes and the Sock Trolls but the King looked confused and before long it was obvious he was no longer listening.

"I'm tired of this. I have better things to do," he said after a while. He really didn't have anything better to do, but he was already thinking about where to move the library so that it was closer to the swimming pool.

"Send them both to the dungeons until they can return my socks," he commanded. Guards appeared out of a nearby doorway and, having learned their lesson yesterday, picked up Princess and Jim only two at a time.

"But how are we supposed to return your socks if we're in a dungeon?" asked Jim.

"Don't you try to confuse me with your tricky logic," said the King. "That's your problem, not mine."

Chapter 9

This dungeon certainly hasn't got any nicer

The palace dungeon hadn't become any nicer in the few hours that Princess and Jim had been away. Nobody had swept the floors, brightened up the place with a little paint or added thoughtful touches like curtains and flowers. The walls were still bare stone and the windows were so high up that a simple toad or snake had no chance of climbing out.

Princess and Jim found themselves together in a small cell with an extremely high ceiling. There was no way to get to the door's keyhole from the inside.

"It doesn't look like we'll be getting out of here again in a hurry," said Jim.

"Sorry that I got us both into this mess," sighed Princess. "If you hadn't asked me to help, neither of us would be here."

"But at least you got to meet the Prince," Jim said brightly. "Wasn't that a lot of fun?"

Meeting the Prince hadn't exactly gone as Princess had intended, and now her dreams of becoming a real princess were fading away. In fact, it looked like most of her dreams were never going to come true. Dungeons are not the kinds of places to have exciting adventures, at least not in this book.

Princess looked at the straw on the floor of the cell. She wondered how long it would take to knit eight thousand socks out of straw, and if the King would let them go if she managed it. Of course, she didn't know how to knit, didn't have any knitting needles, and straw is probably not the best thing to knit with. If you've ever tried to knit anything out of straw, you'll know how difficult it is. And if you're determined to do it, you only end up with really uncomfortable clothes anyway.

As she sat thinking about what to do, she heard a very small voice.

"Excuse me," it said. Princess looked around but couldn't see anything.

"Excuse me," came the voice again. "I have just one small request. Please don't eat me." The voice seemed to be coming from above Princess's head.

There, hanging from the ceiling, was a spider— not a particularly large one but just about the size that a toad might enjoy as a mid-morning snack. Well they might not actually enjoy it—spiders, like most bugs, are not known for their tastiness. You would never go into a sweet shop and ask for quarter of a pound of spiders. Even at Halloween that would be a disgusting idea.

The spider lowered herself down further on her silk thread and landed on the floor beside Princess and Jim. At this point in the story, there are probably two things that could happen.

1. The spider and all her friends spin thousands of socks out of silk, or

2. The spider helps Princess and Jim escape in an extremely unlikely way.

Either way, it's lucky that the spider arrived at this point, otherwise the story might have got really boring (if it isn't already). The rest of the book would be all about a toad and a snake sitting in a dungeon, not doing anything at all. Instead, you're reading about why you don't want to be reading about a toad and a snake sitting in a dungeon.

Anyway, when the King saw the thousands of beautiful socks spun by the spider and her friends, he was so impressed that he immediately released Princess and Jim, threw a huge party in their honour and made the spiders the royal sock spinners. Princess married Prince Glamchaps, became a real princess and lived happily ever after. The end.

Except she didn't, he didn't, they didn't and it isn't, because that's not what happened. Although if you're completely fed up with this story and can't wait for it to end, now would be a good place to stop reading and find something more interesting to do.

If you're still reading, you might want to know what actually happened next.

"I can help you to escape, if you'd like," said Susan. At this point, you're either thinking, "Who on earth is Susan?" or you've worked out that there are only three characters in this cell and that Susan must be the spider. You can tell she's important because I've given her a name quite early on.

If you think it's unfair that lots of other characters in the book didn't get names, don't worry. All the other characters do actually have names and they're at the back of the book so that you can read them whenever you like.

"Of course we'd like to escape," said Princess. "But why would you help us?"

"Because it will annoy the King," said Susan. "The King keeps sweeping my webs up. You wouldn't believe how annoying it is to spend all night on a beautiful web only to have somebody come along with a feather duster in the morning and get rid of it. I happen to think my webs are very pretty."

"All right," nodded Princess, "so how are you going to get us out?"

Susan winked with four of her eight eyes and started to spin a web against the wall of the cell. Then she spun another, and then another. She kept spinning until the wall under the window was covered with shimmering silk.

"Go on, then," she said. "Spider silk is pretty sticky stuff, just ask a fly. You should be able to climb to the window now."

Princess pressed her feet against the wall and found that she could easily walk up it just as easily as standing on the floor.

"That's amazing!" she cried as she reached the top and looked out of the window.

"No, I'm not sure that it is," came a voice from below.

Jim was at the bottom of the wall, trying to climb up but not going anywhere at all. Snakes can twist themselves round almost anything, climb trees, slither through grass and across sand, and many can swim as well as fish do. But snakes don't do so well crossing something sticky, and slithering up a sticky wall turned out to be impossible for Jim.

"I think you're going to have to leave me here," he sighed, after falling off the wall for the eighth time. "There's no way I can get up to that window, and you'll never be able to pull me up."

"I could try," suggested Princess, climbing up onto the window ledge, although she wasn't sure how on earth a toad was supposed to lift a snake.

"There's no point. Why don't you just try and get some help to make that bridge, and then come back for me?" Jim tried to sound brighter than he felt.

"Well, all right. I'll come back for you as soon as I can," Princess agreed, "I'm sure I won't be long."

"No, you're a toad—it's me who's long," said Jim.

Princess climbed out of the window and found herself at the back of the palace, in a field overlooking the King's farmland. The dungeons were right on the edge of the palace so that the dungeon smell didn't put everybody off their tea and cakes. Being so close to freedom also really annoyed the prisoners, which made the King very happy.

"So, what now?" she said to herself. She wasn't going to just run back home and leave Jim in the dungeon, but she had no idea how to come up with a replacement bridge for the gnomes and trolls all by herself.

"Excuse me," said a sheep, wandering up to her, "you're standing on a nice bit of grass there. Could you move?"

Princess hopped to one side and the sheep started munching at the grass where she had been stood. It looked exactly the same as all the other grass for miles around.

To most people, grass is pretty much the same everywhere. Sometimes it's tall, sometimes it's short, and often it's different shades of green, but it's always still grass. To a sheep, though, grass is the most amazing thing ever, and every blade has its own unique flavour. And the grass that tastes

best of all is the grass that somebody else is either eating or standing on. That's why sheep tend to look at you with odd expressions on their faces—they're waiting for you to move. And each sheep is convinced that all the other sheep in the field are keeping the best grass to themselves, which is why they constantly follow each other around, just to make sure.

"Much appreciated," said the sheep as he finished chewing. "You look like you just escaped from that dungeon there. I wouldn't go doing that if I were you, the King won't be pleased at all. Do you happen to have any grass with you?"

"I'm very sorry," said Princess, "but I don't have any grass." She looked around, wondering if the sheep could see the hundreds of acres of grass all around him. "I wonder if I could ask you for some help?" she said.

"You could ask," said the sheep. "I might not say yes, though."

"Well," Princess said, "it might sound odd but I need to knit a bridge for some gnomes and trolls. I'm not sure where to start."

"Really?" asked the sheep. "Knitting a bridge is quite simple. You just need a lot of wool, somebody to spin it and somebody who's good at knitting."

"That does seem fairly obvious," admitted Princess. "Can you spare any wool for me?"

"I'm sure I could spare a bit," nodded the sheep. "You might want to ask the others, too," and he pointed down the hill to a field with about a hundred sheep in it.

Princess spent the rest of the morning (it was still morning, by the way) asking each sheep if they could spare some wool.

The sheep were very happy to give her some wool, as it was a hot day and it was about time they were sheared anyway. Being sheared is certainly better than spending the summer with your wool gradually falling off or being snagged on every fence or hedgerow you pass. It isn't just annoying to have long straggly bits of wool everywhere, it also looks terrible—and sheep are very fashion-conscious.

That's why they ask farmers to spray them with pretty patterns or numbers in reds, blues and other bright colours. Giving some of their wool to a toad comes a close second to being sheared, and it happens more often than you might think.

So, the sheep gathered all their donated wool into one big pile and left it in the corner of their barn, as Princess couldn't carry it all herself.

Princess thanked them kindly, and then hopped towards the palace, hoping to find somebody who could spin the wool into yarn.

There's no way you can knit with wool that's come straight off a sheep. You'd end up with a big pile of wool with knitting needles sticking out of it, and only porcupines or hedgehogs like to dress like that.

Chapter 10

*Don't you think it's about
time for a new chapter?*

Princess hopped into the palace courtyard, hoping that the guards wouldn't be looking for her yet. It seemed like only yesterday that she had last escaped from the dungeon, because it was only yesterday. This time, though, she was on her own.

"You! Toad!" cried a guard. Princess was shocked, partly that the guards were already looking for her, and partly that she hadn't noticed that she'd hopped right up onto a guard's boot.

"Hello," she said in her most innocent voice. "Sorry, I appear to be sitting on your boot."

She hopped down and gave the guard her nicest smile. Toads really aren't very good at smiling, and their nicest smiles tend to look like they've just eaten a very unpleasant beetle. This is usually because they have just eaten a very unpleasant beetle and are trying to persuade themselves that it actually tasted quite nice.

"Why aren't you in the spinning room?" the guard asked. "At this time of day, all toads should be spinning. Get going!" And he pointed towards a door with "Spinning" written across it.

All toads look alike to most people. In fact, all toads look alike to most other toads, which is another reason why they don't normally have names. So, the guard had no idea he was actually talking to the dangerous criminal Princess, and instead he thought that this was just another yarn-spinning toad trying to avoid her work.

Toads don't actually like to spin, even though they're very good at it, so although they'd been used for spinning at the palace for nearly thirty years, a guard always had to stand outside the door to return the ones that really just wanted to do something else.

Now, you might think that Princess being sent to a yarn-spinning room full of toads at exactly the moment that she was looking for somebody to spin her yarn is just the writer being very lazy. You've probably already been thinking about how lucky it was that the spider and the sheep turned up exactly when they did. "That's not very realistic at all," you might be saying.

It might not be like the world that you live in, but I'm sure you don't want to read about Princess walking round the palace asking everybody about how to spin wool into yarn. Sometimes ridiculous things happen just so that we can get on with the story, and maybe Princess was just a very lucky toad.

Princess hopped into the spinning room to find rows of spinning wheels, with a toad sat at each one. A huge pile of wool took up one corner of the room and rolls of yarn were stacked up on shelves near the door.

"Where have you been?" asked a nearby toad as Princess approached.

"That," said Princess, "is a fairly long story. You'd have to read 123 pages just to get to this point. And also, I don't actually work here."

"Then what on earth are you doing here?" asked the toad.

"I could really do with your help," Princess said. "I need a huge pile of wool spinning into yarn. Then it needs to be knitted into a bridge for Sock Gnomes and Sock Trolls."

All the toads in the room stopped spinning, and peered round their wheels at Princess.

"Excuse me?" said the closest toad. "We're already spinning a huge pile of wool into yarn, in case you hadn't noticed. And what on earth is this about a bridge? For gnomes and trolls? Are you quite mad?"

"I don't think so," replied Princess, although at this point she wasn't completely sure. "It really would take a long time to explain, and you'd have to go all the way back to chapter seven to know what was going on. But I can tell you right now that if we get a bridge built for the gnomes and the trolls then the King will get his socks back and he won't need any more socks knitting. I'm guessing that's why you're making so much yarn."

The toads around the room mumbled quietly to each other.

"That's true," one said, "we are spinning yarn to make socks. We've been spinning yarn non-stop for weeks now, trying to keep up with all the socks that are disappearing. If this bridge of yours really does mean that we can have a break, then we'd be happy to help. Even if it does sound completely crazy."

"Thank you! That's amazing," cried Princess. "Although I'm not sure how to get the wool to you. It's quite heavy, you know."

"Don't you worry," said the head toad. "We'll finish our spinning for today and then help you to get it this evening. Even if we have to spin through the night, it'll be worth it if the King stops needing new socks every single day."

"Now I just need to find somebody to do the knitting," Princess said thoughtfully. She had no idea who could knit something as big as a bridge.

"For that," said the head toad, "you'll need elephants. Find them in the knitting room."

It's a little-known fact that elephants are the best and fastest knitters in the world. It may not seem like it, with their huge flat feet and enormous size, but their trunks and tusks make them experts at the job. A knitting elephant will hold both knitting needles in their trunk like chopsticks and use their tusks to hold both the yarn and the finished item.

It's a way of knitting that no other animal or person can do and it is very quick, as long as you don't want anything too small. Elephants are best at knitting blankets and scarves—they find things like gloves far too fiddly. Socks are about the smallest things they can get their tusks into.

Princess slipped out of the spinning room's back door and into a corridor. Luckily there were no guards here, and Princess was able to hop along the hallway until she found a wall full of signs.

The King constantly swapping rooms around didn't just mean that one or two signs were needed, it meant that sometimes entire halls were needed to hold all the signs pointing to every room in the palace. Princess looked for the one saying, "Knitting Room" and eventually found it hidden behind three other signs. It pointed upwards, so Princess found the nearest flight of stairs and started to climb towards the top of the palace.

The stairs led higher and higher, and Princess would have felt that this could not possibly be the right direction if there wasn't a new sign at the top of each flight of steps, still pointing up.

Eventually, right at the very top of the very tallest tower, she came to a door with a sign saying "Knitting" on it. It was clear that this room had been lots of different things in the past as there were hundreds of old room signs crossed out. It seemed that at one point somebody had even tried to put a swimming pool in here.

Inside the room, Princess found thirty elephants crammed into the smallest space that she could imagine fitting thirty elephants. It wasn't something that she had tried to imagine before but if she had, she would have thought about a much larger room.

The elephants looked very uncomfortable in this cramped space, and whoever had decided that this was the best room for knitting had clearly never knitted before. They probably hadn't ever seen an elephant before, either.

Each elephant was busy knitting socks and adding them to a huge pile by the room's only window. A small bird was sorting the socks into pairs and then putting them into a basket attached to a rope. The socks had to be lowered out of the window because there was no way to get them past all the elephants and down the stairs.

"Excuse me," said Princess, "do you think you could help me?"

The elephants hadn't noticed her entering the room, as elephants don't normally pay a lot of attention to toads, and knitting elephants only ever focus on their knitting.

"All the way back down the stairs, large room off the courtyard," said the closest elephant. "Toads belong in the spinning room and you should be there now. Toads don't take up much room, so why you've been given that huge room is beyond me. We have to make do with this tiny space, although at least it's better than being in the coal room like we were yesterday."

The elephant shook his head and clouds of black dust filled the room. The other elephants coughed and tried to keep their newly knitted socks from getting dirty.

"No," answered Princess, "or yes, but no. Yes, I'm a toad, but no, I don't work in the spinning room. I'm trying to get a bridge knitted for Sock Gnomes and Sock Trolls."

If you've read this book from the beginning, you'll already know what's going on with the gnomes, the trolls and the bridge, so you don't need to read about what Princess told the elephants.

If you haven't read the rest of the book and have just jumped in at this point, you must be incredibly confused, so I'll give you a quick summary: Fla-la-la the golden llama has opened the magic bottle of milk on the top of the green mountain, and Rimble the magician has sent her on a mysterious quest to find the purple hoola-hoop and save the people of Bilbury.

Well, actually, none of that has happened—you'll have to go back to the start if you want to find out what's really going on.

And if you have been reading from the start, you're probably now thinking "That story with Fla-la-la and Rimble sounds much more interesting than this one" and you might be right. Still, here we are at the end of chapter ten so we might as well get to the end, otherwise you'll never find out what happens to Princess and if Jim ever gets out of the dungeon.

The elephants eventually agreed to help Princess if it meant that they could stop knitting boring old socks and get onto doing something more interesting.

Elephants are actually very keen on knitting bobble hats and were looking forward to winter so that they could knit hats for all the palace guards. The guards went through hats very quickly, as they put them over the top of their pointy helmets, which tended to rip large holes in them. Most of the guards were not very clever.

So, Princess headed back down the steps and managed to find her way back to the dungeon, following a twisting and turning route which led her from one side of the palace to another.

Nobody had spent any time trying to make the signs around the palace point towards the quickest route to any room, so it always took twice as long to get anywhere as it really needed to. The quickest way to the dungeon might actually have been for Princess to have jumped out in front of a guard and shouted, "Here I am, arrest me!" but then she would have been on the wrong side of the cell door, and she didn't meet any guards on her travels anyway.

"That's great!" said Jim when he heard the news about the toads and the elephants. "It sounds like I'll be out of here in no time at all. And you'll be a free toad. I mean, a properly free toad, not one who's trying to avoid guards all the time."

"Yes, hopefully we can make everybody happy once we get those socks back," replied Princess.

She left Jim talking to Susan the spider, and headed back down to the barn where all her wool was stored, ready for it to be spun and made into the best knitted bridge ever. It was probably going to be the only knitted bridge ever, too.

Chapter 11

Why would anybody make a bridge out of wool?

The toads arrived at the barn just after tea-time, along with the elephants. Princess had no idea how they'd slipped out of the palace without being seen, but she was glad that they were there. The elephants had brought their knitting needles and were also carrying the toads' spinning wheels on their backs.

The sheep gathered around to watch as the toads set up their wheels and began to spin yarn from the huge pile of wool. As the yarn was spun, elephants took hold of it and started to knit, all working on the same part of the bridge at once. It was a very large construction, as it needed to be at least as big as eight thousand socks stitched together.

The sides curved up and made neat hand-rails at the sides, where there was a row of loops for gnome ropes to go through.

The bridge was kind of sheep colour, as there was no time to dye the wool and make it look nice before knitting it. The longer they waited, the longer Jim would be in the dungeon and the more likely it would be that Princess would be caught.

As the evening turned to night, the toads continued to spin and the elephants continued to knit. Princess tried to help but when she tried to spin wool, she ended up producing something that looked like candy floss. She also tried to do some knitting, but only managed to get herself all tangled up. It took six toads twenty minutes to get her free. In the end, it was better that she didn't try to help, so she sat down on the finished end of the bridge and fell fast asleep.

Princess woke in the morning to find the elephants and toads marching back up the field looking very tired and ready for bed. Princess waved and shouted "Thank you!" as they left.

Two elephants had stayed in the barn with Princess, as they knew that a single toad couldn't lift an entire bridge. Princess was very glad they were there, as this story would have gone on a lot longer if she had to find somebody else to carry the bridge.

"Now, where's this gnome village?" said Hannibal, the largest elephant.

"It's in the forest on the other side of the palace," replied Princess, "but it won't take long to get there. If you can lift the bridge, I'll sit up on top and direct you."

"No problem at all," said the other elephant, who was called William.

Both Hannibal and William lifted the bridge up with their trunks and placed it across their backs, with Princess sat on top. Then they set off up the field, walking in step with each other.

The plan was to go around the palace rather than through it, so that they wouldn't be seen, but as they reached the bottom of the palace gardens they saw Prince Glamchaps approaching on his horse. Princess climbed underneath the bridge and hid.

"Woah there!" exclaimed the Prince. "What's going on here? That's a lot of knitting that you're carrying. Aren't you palace elephants? I suspect that something very suspicious and naughty is going on."

"Not at all," replied Hannibal. "This is—umm—"

"This is my scarf," said William, quickly. "It seems to have stretched a bit, so we're—umm—"

"We're taking it down to the river to wash it so that it shrinks," said Hannibal.

"Well," said the Prince thoughtfully, "that seems like a very sensible thing to do, although it hardly seems worth it. It's not very colourful, is it?" He rode up to the elephants and looked closely at the bridge.

"It's just a bit dirty, that's all," said William, "We'll get it nice and clean in the river."

The Prince wondered whether he should go with the elephants to make sure they were telling the truth. But then he remembered that it was almost time for his second breakfast and he hadn't had any jam toast for nearly half an hour.

"Well, have a nice time," he said, trotting off up the garden.

Princess waited a good few minutes before climbing out from underneath the bridge.

"That was close!" she said. "Let's get going—the gnome village is straight down there." And she pointed into the nearby forest.

The elephants had no problem crashing through the brambles, which completely failed to scratch them at all, and soon they saw toadstools growing amongst the trees. The further into the forest they went, the more careful the elephants had to be to avoid crushing any gnome toadstools. This is not easy to do when you're carrying a bridge.

They arrived in the centre of the gnome village and were met by a large crowd of gnomes and trolls. Gee and Tee stepped forwards and peered at the elephants.

"What on earth is this?" asked Gee, looking up to Princess. "First you come to our village with a snake, then you tell us that guards are on the way, and now you turn up with two elephants wearing a dressing gown."

"Maybe we should have just thrown you into the gorge," said Tee. "It seems like it would have saved a lot of trouble."

"If you'd have done that then you wouldn't have a nice new bridge," said Princess, and the elephants pulled the knitting off their backs and laid it at Gee and Tee's feet.

"No thank you," said Tee. "We've already got one. And it looks a lot nicer than that."

"What?" cried Princess. "You promised that if I brought you a new bridge, you'd return the King's socks. Well, here's your new bridge. You should keep your side of the bargain!"

Gee and Tee looked at the elephant's bridge, and then turned to their sock bridge.

"We like our bridge better," they said together. "It's much more colourful and it's much less work to just keep the one we've got."

"But—" Princess was shocked. All that work had been for nothing!

If she had known a little more about gnomes and trolls then she would have known that, as excellent liars, gnomes and trolls don't often keep their word. They think nothing of telling you that they're going to do one thing and then they'll do

exactly the opposite. If a gnome tells you the way to the library, head the other way because you're more likely to get there than if you follow the gnome's directions. If a troll tells you that his name is Barry, you can bet that it's more likely to be something like Mary, or Belinda.

"Should we just stomp his village to pieces?" suggested Hannibal.

"No!" cried Princess. "That might make us all feel better, but it's not a very nice thing to do. You wouldn't like it if the gnomes and trolls stomped your house to bits."

"I'd like to see them try, though," Hannibal said.

"I've got a better idea," said William. "Let's show them that our bridge is much better than theirs. I'm sure they'll want the best bridge."

"If your bridge really is better," said Gee, "then you can have your socks back. But you'll need to prove it."

"No problem," smiled Princess, confident that the elephant's bridge would be up to the task. "Let's put it up."

So, the gnomes and trolls hammered in some new posts at each side of the gorge, next to the sock bridge. Some new ropes were

hauled out and attached to the elephant bridge, and then the whole thing was strung across the gap. Soon both bridges were swinging side by side in the breeze.

"To prove that your bridge is better," said Tee, "you must send an elephant across it."

The elephants and Princess looked at each other, slightly worried. They had built the bridge to carry gnomes and trolls, and if you read page 60, you'll know that gnomes and trolls are not very big. At least, not in this story. I'm sure you've come across other stories where trolls are huge monsters but I wouldn't have been able to fit them in the book if they were that big.

"It's the only way we're going to get the socks," pointed out Hannibal. "I'll do it." And he stepped out onto the new bridge as gently as he could.

Elephants don't normally tread very gently, even when they're trying to be quiet, so the bridge bent downwards as soon as Hannibal stepped onto it.

"Keep going!" shouted the gnomes and trolls, thrilled that they might get to see an elephant fall into a gorge. It's not a very nice thing to get excited about, but it's the kind of thing that gnomes and trolls find entertaining.

Hannibal kept walking, slowly at first and then faster and faster as he tried to get to the other side. The bridge bent lower and lower until...

Nothing happened. It stayed together and Hannibal reached the other side with a triumphant blow on his trunk.

"There you go! You can give us the socks now," cried Princess.

"Wait just one minute!" said Gee. "One elephant is easy. You could stand one elephant on our smallest toadstool. You could lift one elephant with a teaspoon. You could blow one elephant over with a gust of wind."

I did say that gnomes were excellent liars.

"You must walk TWO elephants across the bridge," announced Gee.

"And a toad," added Tee.

Gee and Tee were hoping that both elephants and Princess would fall down into the gorge and the gnomes and trolls would be left in peace.

Nobody would ask them to give the socks back and they'd get to keep whatever was left of the other bridge.

"No!" cried Hannibal, William and Princess together.

"Yes!" cried all the gnomes and trolls.

Hannibal, William and Princess could see that they had no choice. They couldn't just grab the sock bridge with hundreds of gnomes and trolls around, and they didn't want to return to the palace without the socks.

So, Hannibal set off from the far side of the bridge, and William and Princess set off from their side towards the middle.

The rope creaked and the posts sounded like they might break at any minute. The knitted bridge bent alarmingly low, so low that both elephants disappeared below the edge of the gorge and the gnomes and trolls had to line up along the edge to see them.

With every step they took, the bridge got lower and lower, tighter and tighter, and the ropes creaked more and more. Gee seemed very disappointed. "I can't believe the bridge hasn't broken!" he grumbled.

Indeed, it hadn't. Both elephants and Princess were stood right in the middle, swaying a little but showing no signs of falling. They walked together to the troll side of the bridge, and stepped onto solid ground with huge grins on their faces.

"There!" shouted Princess. "We've done it! You HAVE to give us the socks now, unless you want to join us on the bridge."

"No thank you," mumbled Tee.

"Not so fast, though," shouted Gee. "You haven't proved that your bridge is stronger! Our sock bridge might be just as strong. Come back together over our bridge."

Of course, Gee knew that the sock bridge couldn't hold two elephants and a toad. He knew that it would break as soon as they stepped onto it, and they'd end up tumbling into the gorge. And then the gnomes and trolls would be left with the elephant's strong bridge—they couldn't lose!

"What choice do we have?" asked William. "I don't see a way out of this."

"It's not really a choice," sighed Princess. "If the sock bridge breaks then it proves that ours is better. We'll get the socks, but we'll be at the bottom of the gorge. If the sock bridge doesn't break then it doesn't prove anything. They won't give us the socks."

"So, we'll have to make sure that it breaks," said Hannibal. "Hold onto me!" And he set foot onto the sock bridge, holding tight onto the rope.

"Sounds good to me," nodded William as he grabbed hold of Hannibal's tail and followed him onto the bridge.

"You're both mad!" cried Princess, clinging tight to William's tail.

The bridge creaked and bent below them, and stitches started to break all around.

"This is completely crazy! We're going to fall!" Princess shouted in a panic. She didn't know what to do. The other side of the gorge was too far away for even a toad to jump.

William tossed his head to the left and right, and as he did so his tusks caught the ropes near the edge of the bridge.

The ropes twanged and twinged as threads snapped. Suddenly both the ropes holding the bridge broke at the same time. Princess, Hannibal and William found themselves tumbling down faster and faster, surround by falling socks and broken rope.

Chapter 12

The chapter that's nearly, but
not quite, at the end

"This is the end!" cried Princess as they fell further and further down into the gorge.

"No, it isn't," Hannibal shouted. "There's still one more chapter to go!"

He was still holding onto one of the ropes with his trunk. This rope was attached to a post on the gnome side of the gap, and the elephants and Princess swung towards the steep side of the gorge.

"Get ready for a big bump!" shouted William as they swung closer and closer to the wall. It had only taken a couple of seconds, but to Princess everything seemed to be happening in slow motion.

WHAM! The two elephants and Princess hit the wall of the gorge and Princess was sure that they were going to fall. Somehow Hannibal kept his grip on the rope and William held tight onto his tail.

"Well, that was fun," said Hannibal calmly, and he started to walk up the side of the gorge, twisting the rope around his tusks and pulling with his trunk.

If you've never seen an elephant climb up a gorge wall using a rope, you'll find it difficult to imagine what it looked like. Princess really was not enjoying the experience at all but at least it was better than being at the bottom of the gorge.

The gnomes and trolls peered over the edge in amazement.

"Wait a minute," shouted Gee, "that's cheating!"

"You can't do that," complained Tee.

But they could. After a couple of minutes, two slightly bruised elephants and a very shocked toad climbed over the edge of the gorge and stood by the tattered bridge. The gnomes and trolls didn't know what to say.

"Your bridge seems to be broken," said William.

"We might as well take these, then," added Hannibal, pulling the remains of the sock bridge up by the rope.

Gee and Tee couldn't think of anything wise to say, and they didn't have any excuses left to stop the elephants from taking the socks. Instead, they just stood with mouths open wide while Hannibal and William packed the socks up on their backs, and Princess made sure that the last few threads were undone from the bridge posts.

"Goodbye!" called Princess as she climbed up on Hannibal's back, and the three of them set off together through the village. A few gnomes started to wave as they left, but then thought better of it.

"Well, that was easy," smiled Hannibal, but Princess was fairly sure that 'easy' wasn't the word she would use.

Soon they were back at the palace gardens. It was about lunch-time so everybody had gone inside for something to eat. Hannibal, William and Princess were able to march right up the gardens, past the washing lines and to the edge of the courtyard.

"So, what should we do with all these socks?" asked William. "I'm not sure we can just knock on the door and hand them to the King. He won't believe where they came from."

"And if he does," said Hannibal, "he'll be extremely angry with the gnomes and the trolls. He might even flatten their village to punish them."

"However cruel they were to us, we can't let that happen," said Princess. "But I've got another idea."

Arriving back at the dungeon window, Princess climbed back down the spider-silk wall and dropped to the cell floor. Jim and Susan were surprised to see her.

"Princess!" cried Jim. "What are you doing here? If you didn't get the socks then it looks like I'm stuck here forever."

"Don't worry about that!" smiled Princess, as thousands of socks came tumbling down into the cell. They were all still stitched together but the elephants had bent the window bars back to squeeze them through. When the last socks had landed on the floor, there was very little room in the cell for anything else.

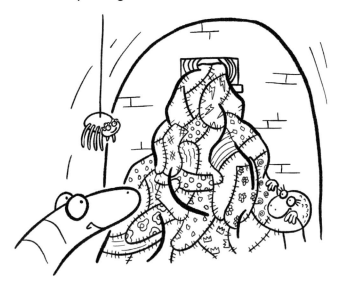

"Thank you!" called Princess, and the two elephants waved their trunks. They bent the bars back and headed off to get some well-earned rest.

"What's going on?" Jim asked. "How did you get the socks back? And what on earth are we going to do with them?"

"I'll tell you while we get these unstitched," Princess said, and she started to pick at the threads holding the socks together.

Jim joined in, using his teeth and his tail to remove threads as quickly as he could. Susan helped as much as possible, but spiders aren't much good with any threads apart from their own. Meanwhile, Princess told them all about what had happened since she left the cell.

I don't need to tell you what she said because that would be like reading the last three chapters all over again. If you do want the full experience, then you can go back to page 113 and read it again if you like. It might be a bit boring, though, because you already know what's going to happen.

Princess, Jim and Susan worked all afternoon and all through the night to finish the job. Nobody came near the dungeon cell as prisoners were only allowed one meal a day, and that's if they were very lucky.

Eventually all the socks looked like socks again, rather than part of a huge gnome bridge. A few of the socks had holes in them and most of them needed a good wash, as gnomes and trolls had spent a whole day walking backwards and forwards over them.

"Well, I'm glad that's all done," said Jim. "I wouldn't want to have to do that again."

"No," said Princess. "Hopefully nobody will ever have to do that again, although I do feel a bit bad for undoing all the hard work that the gnomes put into this."

Jim was surprised. "Really? They stole these socks from the King, so they should never have been stitching them together in the first place."

"Yes, but the King stole many of them from the people and animals in his kingdom," said Princess. "I hope that he gives them back when we return them."

"And how are we going to do that, anyway?" asked Jim.

Just then they heard footsteps in the corridor, and a clanking sound from the door.

"Here you go," said the dungeon guard as he unlocked the door, "it's breakfast time."

The guard walked into the room and looked around. He stared for a minute.

"What on earth?" he said, and dropped the bowl of turnip and stewed apple soup that he was carrying. He ran out of the cell, stopping only to lock the door behind him.

Soon there was the sound of many feet coming towards Princess and Jim's cell. As the door was opened, it turned out that those feet were attached to people, and one of those people was the King.

"My socks!" he cried, seeing the huge pile taking up the entire cell. He walked over to the socks and picked up a few to see if they were real. Then he turned to Princess.

"So, you finally came to your senses and decided to give them back," he said.

The King was not very clever, and to him it made perfect sense that a toad could have hidden eight thousand socks in a dungeon cell. He didn't even think about how she might have got them there in the first place.

"Of course I didn't have your socks!" cried Princess. "But Jim and I have managed to get them back for you, even though you locked us in the dungeon."

The King scratched his head for a minute. "Well, I don't see how you could have found my socks when you were stuck in here. I think you had them with you all the time. You and that snake, there."

"That's impossible!" complained Jim, but the King wasn't listening.

"I don't want to hear another word," he commanded. "Guards, get these two into an empty cell. And get those socks back to where they belong."

And with that, the King swept out of the cell and up the dungeon stairs.

"Was this part of your plan?" asked Jim.

"No, not really," said Princess.

The two of them were moved into another cell which looked exactly the same except that it wasn't full of socks. They watched through the bars as an army of creatures—mice, beavers and goats—carried the socks away back into the palace. It seemed like all the trouble they had gone to was for nothing, and they would both spend the rest of their days in this dungeon.

"I don't understand it," said Jim. "We got the socks back—well, you did most of it—and it's obvious that we can't have been hiding them in the cell. Why won't the King even listen to us?"

"I don't know," said Princess, thoughtfully. "He's still as bad-tempered as he was when he didn't know where his socks were. It really does look like we're stuck here."

"But that can't be the end of the story," complained Jim. "There's still one more chapter left in this book, and I can't imagine that it'll just be about how miserable we are."

"No, that would be a really boring way to end a book," agreed Princess. "Something exciting must be going to happen otherwise nobody will even bother to finish reading."

Just then, Prince Glamchaps burst through the door of their cell.

Chapter 13

Let's hope everybody lives happily ever after

Obviously when I say that Prince Glamchaps burst through the door, I don't mean that he ripped the door apart and came leaping through the pieces, even though that would be extremely dramatic and would probably look very good in a movie.

I mean that he unlocked and opened the door, then stepped through the doorway. That doesn't sound very exciting, though, so you can see why I would just write that he burst through the door, even if it's not strictly true. Of course, now I've ruined the drama and excitement by explaining it.

Anyway, there stood Prince Glamchaps, looking down at the shocked toad and snake with a big grin on his face.

"You found the socks!" he cried. "I don't know how you did it, and I don't care! You're both heroes!"

And he picked up Princess and Jim and gave them a hug which knocked the breath out of both of them.

"Well," gasped Princess, "this day is finally starting to get a bit better."

"Ugh," said Jim. Like most snakes, he wasn't a fan of being hugged. Some snakes, like the Boa Constrictor, are very keen on giving hugs, but that's a whole different story and not something I'm going to get into here.

"Ignore my father," continued the Prince, putting Princess and Jim back down. "He's spent so much of his life worrying about what he's wearing on his feet that he's gone sock crazy. I'm here to set you free, although I suspect that you may already have found your way to freedom before." He gave them both a smile and a knowing wink.

"And of course, I know that the Sock Gnomes took the socks," he went on. "That's pretty obvious, but it never occurred to the King, and I didn't want to tell him because he'd get so angry that he'd have his elephants trample all over their toadstools."

"It's no less than they deserve," Jim said. Having met them and heard about what they tried to do to Princess, Hannibal and William, he was not at all sure he liked gnomes or trolls.

"I'm sure they're not as mean as they seem," said Princess, "and even if they are, nobody deserves to be squashed."

"Exactly," agreed the Prince. "I had hoped that eventually the King would give up on the idea of socks, but that clearly didn't happen. So, it's just as well he ended up getting them back, and however you managed to get them for him, well done."

He beckoned to Princess and Jim, "Now, please will you come with me?"

And he led the pair out of the cell and up the dungeon stairs into the palace.

They passed through both large and small chambers, along corridors and finally came to the throne room, where all the socks had been piled. All the King's single socks had also been brought down from the various drawers and piled up in the same hall, and a team of small birds was busily trying to match them up into pairs. As Princess and Jim watched, the pile of socks shook and swayed, and then the King burst out of it again dressed only in his underpants. He was swimming and diving playfully through the socks, singing a song about Sock Heaven and about Sock Mermaids floating in a sea of socks.

"I think it's probably time I took over running the kingdom," said Prince Glamchaps thoughtfully. "The King may have finally lost his marbles."

"He doesn't appear to be completely with it," agreed Jim as the King started turning somersaults above the socks, landing on his bottom and giggling playfully.

"He does seem happy, though," Princess said.

"I may need your help, though," said Prince Glamchaps.

And that could be a whole story all by itself, but as this is the last chapter in the book, there's really no room to tell it. So, I'll just tell you briefly what happened, leaving out all the little details like what colour the seven-hundredth pair of socks were, or what Jim had for breakfast on the third day.

The socks were eventually all paired together and those that needed mending were darned by the elephants, who now had a lot more spare time. Then all the socks were given a very thorough wash (Sock Gnomes and Sock Trolls do not always smell very nice) and they were sorted by size, colour and texture. With the help of Princess and Jim, who were now sock experts, they were shared out amongst the King and all the people and animals in the kingdom.

The King was happy to have his favourite pairs back, and he spent most of his days admiring them in his special new sock room. His kingdom was still peaceful, so he really didn't need to do very much, and Prince Glamchaps ran things from day to day anyway.

This made everybody very happy, as the Prince was much nicer than his father. He also didn't tend to wander around in his underwear and make everybody feel slightly uncomfortable. He made sure that some very nice socks were sent to the Sock Gnomes and Sock Trolls each month, just to keep them from stealing any more.

Jim was made Royal Keeper of Socks and all Sock-Like Things, which was a grand title for a job that mostly involved doing whatever he liked all day. This suited Jim very well because the job came with very little risk of being thrown in a dungeon again.

Princess became very good friends with the Prince, and he found her advice valuable as she helped him to run the kingdom. They grew closer each day, and together they did good deeds and made the kingdom a happier place to live for everybody.

One day, after a few seasons had come and gone, and lots of important things had happened that I don't have room to tell you about, the Prince got down on one knee. Then he got a bit further down until his nose was almost touching the ground (because toads are not very tall) and said, "Princess, will you marry me and become a real princess?"

Princess thought for a while and said, "That's a lovely thing to ask, but no thank you. I've enjoyed being at the palace all this time, and I'm very fond of you, but I think I'd rather just stay a normal toad. I'm very good at being a toad, and being a real princess seems like a job for somebody else."

So, although Princess had always dreamed about marrying a prince, she decided that she would return to her pond and do what she could to help out her fellow toads instead. All the people and animals gathered together at the palace gates and waved her goodbye.

"I'll miss you," said Jim, "although I don't know why. Your pond is only about half an hour's walk from the palace."

"Yes, that's a good point," agreed Princess. "Maybe I'll pop back and see you all from time to time."

"I'd like that," said the Prince, "and if you change your mind about becoming a real princess, just let me know."

"I'll think about it," nodded Princess.

When Princess arrived back at the pond, her first job was to give everybody names, even if they thought they didn't need them. Without names, the toads hadn't realised they were each very special, and they had been satisfied to just sit around and eat disgusting bugs.

Princess showed them all the amazing things that were out in the world beyond the pond, and regularly visited the palace with her friends. To the toads, Princess became a real princess, and nobody ever made fun of her name again.

The End

The bit at the back of the book

Things that I made up— they're not true at all

- Snakes can't really pick locks. They don't have the patience and few sakes have any real reason to pick locks anyway (page 27).

- Pelicans are not good at carrying washing. One slip and they'd swallow your pants whole (page 29).

- Owls are not stupid. They really can't read or do maths but they are quite intelligent as far as birds go (page 32).

- The vast majority of mice do not read and they cannot do sums (page 33).

- Giraffes do not hang washing out to dry. Putting washing on a giraffe will probably mean it stays there a very long time, as they're much more likely to forget about it than hang it out to dry for you (page 40).

- Mice do not sort out socks and they're not very neat. They really will chew up your socks to make a bed and then use the corner of your drawer as a toilet. Trust me on this (page 47).

- Sock Gnomes are not real. Sorry but it's your washing machine that eats those socks (page 53).

- There is no gnome-catching contest in Sweden. See 'Sock Gnomes are not real' above (page 58).

- Brambles do not deliberately dig their thorns into people. They just do it without any thinking at all (page 61).

- Toadstools don't grow big enough to get inside. That's quite a shame, actually (page 63).

- Sock Trolls are not real either. But they really should be (page 69).

- Snakes don't get bad backs from sleeping on cheap mattresses. At least, not as far as we know. Snakes are not very talkative (page 101).

- Sheep don't normally ask farmers to spray them because they think it will look good. Farmers spray sheep to keep track of which sheep is which. Sheep end to look pretty much alike (page 117).

- Hedgehogs and porcupines are not really very fashion-conscious. Any clothes they try on tend to just get ripped to pieces (page 118).

- Toads don't spin wool into yarn. Nobody knows if that's because they can't do it or if they just don't want to do it (page 121).

- Elephants can't really knit. Holding knitting needles like chopsticks really isn't the way to do it, and most elephants don't like wearing knitted clothes (page 125).

- It's not really a good idea to make bridges out of wool, which is why you don't see many wool bridges. A wool bridge probably wouldn't support two elephants (page 133).

Things that are most definitely true

- Most toads don't have names. If you want to name a toad, though, you should go ahead—they won't mind (page 1).

- Bugs are, in general, disgusting. Although some people do eat them and if you cover ants in chocolate they taste a little less disgusting (page 4).

- Toads do not taste very nice, which is why most predators won't eat them. A few snakes eat the venomous ones for their venom, but that's a whole different story (page 6).

- Toads don't wear socks. Neither do snakes (page 8).

- Goats are not good at doing laundry. Please don't even try (page 44).

- Sock Gnomes cannot grow beards. See 'Sock Gnomes are not real' above (page 56).

- Many wild Toadstools and mushrooms are poisonous. If you find one growing in the woods or your garden, don't eat it as you could end up being very ill indeed. You are not a gnome (page 87).

- Most spiders have eight eyes. I don't think they can wink, but it would be quite a lot of effort for them if they could (page 111).

The names of all the characters that you thought didn't have names

If you're really concerned about names then you might want to know that the guards were called Eddie, Waylon, Marcus, Mathia, Jonathan, Carl, Hadley, Kelvin, Winston, Trenton, Mario, Sullivan, Jett, Walker, Sean, Preston, Jamir, Cole, Jakob and Jamie.

The pelicans in the laundry were called Kelly, Tia, Lilah, Cory and Joanna. Terry's mouse was called Lucie.

The goat who carried the washing was called Julie, the pigeon who lit the candle was Charles, the mice who tidied the socks were Michael and Sally and the pelicans were Misty, Florence and Billy.

The giraffes, beavers and birds were Henry, Rosie, Hilda, Frank, Oscar and George. The sheep was called Brian, and all the other sheep in the field were called Martin (yes, all of them—even the girls).

The toads in the spinning room really didn't have names but you can call them anything you like. Toad 1, 2, 3, 4 and so on is fine.

The elephants were called Frankie, Henry, Julie, Helen, Rosemary, Dee, Ginger, Ewan, Bert, Oswald, Matthew, Sue, Benjamin, Franklin, Jude, Jane, Neve, Crystal, Annette, Archimedes, Dumbo, Grant, Clarissa, Darlene, Frosty, Hollie, Tobias and Misty. The elephant's bird was called Gruber.

The gnomes were called Mark, Tony, Ginger, Marigold, Hollie, Bart, Astrid, Ursula, Heather, Hazel, Mitchell, Ruth, Simon, Grant, Helen, Tandi, Yasmin, Isabel, William, Thomas, Isla, Pat, Quentin, Reuben, Tilda, Christopher, Violet, Brian, Paul, Ernie, Zack, Priscilla, Liam, Katherine,

Jane, Fred, Owen, Walter, Anne, Francis, Alexander, Toby, Ryan, Derek, Rupert, Orville, Parsley, Clarissa, Rebekah, Xander, Graham, Sarah, Penny and Naomi. Yes, there were girl gnomes in the story—they wear fake beards too. The rest of the gnomes were called Gnome or "Hey, you".

The trolls were all called Donald. Don't ask.